AUTHOR'S NOTE

Won Ton and Chopstick is told in a series of senryu (SEN-ree-yoo), a form of Japanese poetry developed from and similar to haiku (HI-koo). Both senryu and haiku feature three unrhymed lines containing a maximum of seventeen syllables (5-7-5, respectively); each form also captures the essence of a moment. In haiku, that moment focuses on nature. In senryu, the foibles of human nature—or in this case, feline and canine nature—are the focus, expressed by a narrator in a humorous, playful, or ironic way.

Bashō is the pseudonym of Matsuo Munefusa (1644–1694), the Japanese haiku master.

For my agent, Ginger Knowlton,
and my editor, Sally Doherty,
with purrs of gratitude

—L. W.

To my boys, Isaac and Ezra

—E. Y.

Henry Holt and Company, LLC
Publishers since 1866
175 Fifth Avenue
New York, New York 10010
mackids.com

Library of Congress Cataloging-in-Publication Data
Wardlaw, Lee.
Won Ton and Chopstick : a cat and dog tale told in haiku / Lee Wardlaw ; illustrated by Eugene Yelchin. — First edition.
pages   cm
Sequel to: Won Ton, a cat tale told in haiku.
Summary: Won Ton and his boy are enjoying a fine life until "Doom" arrives—a dog that is smelly and steals his dinner, but soon the disgruntled cat learns that his new family member might have some good points, too.
ISBN 978-0-8050-9987-4 (hardback)
[1. Dog adoption—Fiction. 2. Dogs—Fiction. 3. Cats—Fiction. 4. Haiku. 5. Humorous stories.]
I. Yelchin, Eugene, illustrator. II. Title.
PZ7.W2174Wok 2015   [E]—dc23   2014014074

Henry Holt books may be purchased for business or promotional use. For information on bulk purchases, please contact Macmillan Corporate and Premium Sales Department at (800) 221-7945 x5442 or by e-mail at specialmarkets@macmillan.com.

First Edition—2015
The artist used graphite and gouache on watercolor paper to create the illustrations for this book.
Printed in China by Macmillan Production Asia Ltd., Kowloon Bay, Hong Kong (vendor code: 10)

1 3 5 7 9 10 8 6 4 2

WON TON
and
CHOPSTICK

A Cat and Dog Tale Told in Haiku

Lee Wardlaw

illustrated by Eugene Yelchin

Henry Holt and Company

New York

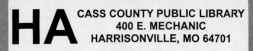

The Routine

It's a fine life, Boy.

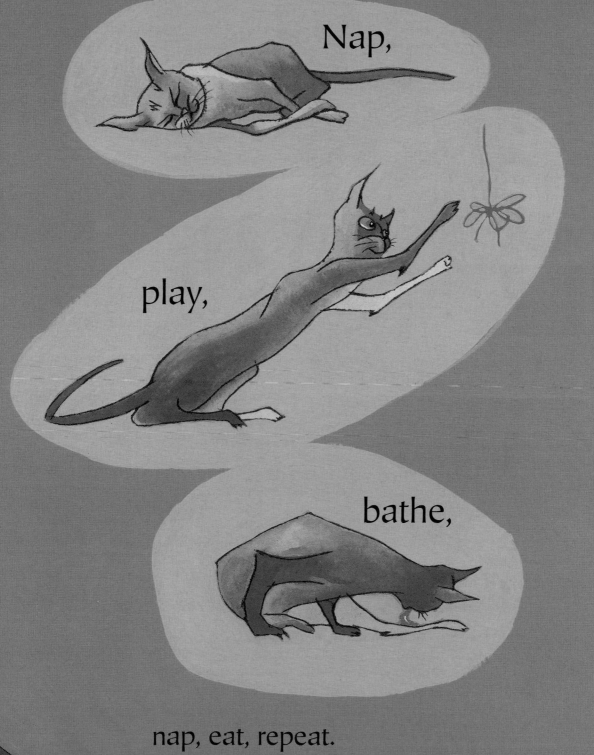

Nap,

play,

bathe,

nap, eat, repeat.
Practice makes purrfect.

The Sneaking Suspicion

Yawn. Who dares disturb
my beauty snooze? Duty calls!
Must snoop before snack.

Proper cats prefer
playthings with feathers or fur.
So whose toys are these?

Curious. This door
is *never* closed. Perhaps *yowl*
is the magic word?

The Surprise

Ears perk. Fur prickles.
Belly low, I creep . . . peek . . . *FREEZE!*
My eyes full of Doom.

Master of escape!
High-flying, dog-defying
acrobatic cat!

Puthimoutputhim
outputhimoutputhim—wait!
I said *him*, not *me*!

The Naming

Sis goes first: "Sushi,
Cookie, Noodle, Scraps." Great Rats!
It's a *dog*, not lunch.

Brutus? Ninja? *FANG*?
Cats don't laugh, Boy, but I might
make an exception.

Chopstick! Why not Fork,
Spoon, or Spatula? Dumb pup
wags no matter what.

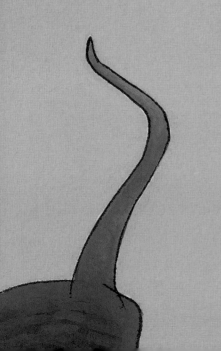

Don't bother barking
your real name. I've already
guessed. It must be . . . Pest!

The Rules

Hey, Pest! Heed my hiss!
My blankie. *My* bowl. *My* boy.
Trespassers bitten.

The Altercation

Who. Ate. My. Dinner.
Your eyes say "no-no," but your
breath brags of tuna.

Keep your distance, Pest!
I've five compelling reasons—
and that's just *one* paw!

Puthimoutputhim
outputhimoutputhim—wait!
I said *him*, not *me*!

The Banishment

Picket fence lament:
Woe is *meeee*-ow! The crowd howls.
Cue for an encore.

Pounced a plump mouse but
set him free. Just not hungry.
Maybe tomorrow.

Alone, Q-curled tight.
Night is cold without you, Boy,
despite my fur coat.

The Adjustment

Yes, my bowl is clean.
Morsels, fishy-fresh. I guess
I'm still not hungry.

If I huddle here
in shadow, will Boy forget
to send me away?

Bathroom skirmish ends
in triumph! Boredom subdued—
and I can blame you.

Puthimoutputhim
outputhimoutputhim—wait!
I said *him,* not *us!*

The Vindication

Chew toy lost its squeak?
Why not gnaw this shoe instead?
I'm sure Boy won't mind.

TULIPS

New bone to bury?
Soil's much softer over there.
I'm sure Mom won't mind.

Play chase with you? *Yawn.*
Why not ask some other cat?
No! Stop! Never mind . . .

The Bath

Towel, brush, tub o' suds.
Such a lot of fuss and muss
to still smell like dog.

I am self-cleaning.
Watch: easy as one, two, three—
even with eyes closed!

Licklicklicklicklick
lick—Great Rats! You touched me! Now
I must start over.

The Rainy Day

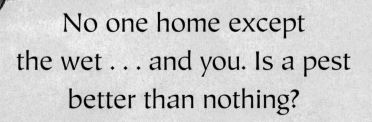

No one home except
the wet . . . and you. Is a pest
better than nothing?

You shouldn't rummage
through the rubbish. But what's done
is done, so . . . let's eat!

I play with balls, too!
But much smaller, less slobber.
And I *never* fetch.

Great Rats! It's only
thunder! Who knew you were a
scaredy cat? (Like me.)

Breaking news: YOU SNORE.
Twitch and whimper, too. Yet you
make a soft pillow.

Harmony
(Usually)

Belly pounce. Nose lick.
Whisker-kiss. Ha! Can't escape
furry alarm clocks!

My chin requests Boy's
skillful fingers. In return,
symphony of purr.

Some parts of *woof* I
will never understand. But . . .
practice makes purrfect.

Your secret revealed.
What kind of name is Bashō?
I shall call you . . . Friend.